Come Back, Come Back, Wherever You Are

by Arthur Laurents

SAMUELFRENCH.COM

MUSIC USE NOTE

Licensees are solely responsible for obtaining formal written permission from copyright owners to use copyrighted music in the performance of this play and are strongly cautioned to do so. If no such permission is obtained by the licensee, then the licensee must use only original music that the licensee owns and controls. Licensees are solely responsible and liable for all music clearances and shall indemnify the copyright owners of the play and their licensing agent, Samuel French, Inc., against any costs, expenses, losses and liabilities arising from the use of music by licensees.

IMPORTANT BILLING AND CREDIT REQUIREMENTS

All producers of *COME BACK, COME BACK, WHEREVER YOU ARE* must give credit to the Author of the Play in all programs distributed in connection with performances of the Play, and in all instances in which the title of the Play appears for the purposes of advertising, publicizing or otherwise exploiting the Play and/or a production. The name of the Author *must* appear on a separate line on which no other name appears, immediately following the title and *must* appear in size of type not less than fifty percent of the size of the title type.

In addition the following credit *must* be given in all programs and publicity information distributed in association with this piece:

Premiere Production Presented by
George Street Playhouse
David Saint, Artistic Director Todd Schmidt, Managing Director

COME BACK, COME BACK, WHEREVER YOU ARE was first produced by the George Street Playhouse (David Saint, artistic director; Todd Schmidt, managing director) in New Brunswick, New Jersey on October 9, 2009. The performance was directed by Arthur Laurents, with sets by James Youmans, costumes by Esther Arroyo, lighting by Howell Binkley, sound by Christopher J. Bailey, and musical direction by Christopher Howatt. The production stage manager was Thomas Clewell. The cast was as follows:

SARA	Alison Fraser
DOUGAL	Jim Bracchitta
MARION	Shirley Knight
RICHARD	John Carter
MICHELLE	Leslie Lyles

CHARACTERS

Sara
Dougal
Marion
Richard
Michelle

ACT ONE

Scene One

(Darkness. Fading in, a piano and bass backing **SARA** *singing a melancholy tinged* **Life Is Just a Bowl of Cherries***. As her voice fades in, a spot on her fades in. She is wearing a simple black summery dress.)*

SARA.

Life is just a bowl of cherries.

Don't take it serious, it's too mysterious.

You work, you slave, you worry so

but when the end comes around,

you've got to go go go.

So keep repeating it's the berries.

The strongest oak must fall.

The great things in life to you were just loaned

so how can you lose what you've never owned.

(She stops for a moment. The bass continues to pluck away. Then she comes back in:)

Life is just a bowl of cherries,

so live and laugh,

laugh and love,

live and love and laugh at it all."

(There is applause which fades out as the light does. Darkness. Then light comes up on a back door in an alleyway. A man is waiting: **DOUGAL***. He is 40 something, younger than Sara, dressed casually, as attractive as his easy chatter. But like her song, there is something sad there.* **SARA** *comes out the door, a little jacket over the dress and carrying a purse. The mutual sexual attraction is unacknowledged.)*

DOUGAL. Welcome back.

SARA. Thank you.

DOUGAL. I'd just about given up on hearing you again. When I asked that blowhard doorman who acts as though he owns the place –

SARA. He does.

DOUGAL. He does?

SARA. He does.

DOUGAL. You like him?

SARA. I wouldn't sing here if I didn't.

DOUGAL. Well, this hasn't been my year anyway. When I asked him if you were ever coming back, he said he didn't know.

SARA. He didn't. Neither did I.

DOUGAL. You didn't?

SARA. No.

DOUGAL. That doesn't make sense.

SARA. Maybe not but I didn't know.

DOUGAL. Why not?

SARA. You don't know me well enough to ask.

DOUGAL. I know you better than you think. You're a very personal singer and I've heard you sing a lot. You're singing very differently now.

SARA. Yes, I am.

DOUGAL. I like it.

SARA. That's nice to hear.

DOUGAL. It suits how I'm feeling these days.

SARA. *(smiles)* And how are you feeling these days?

DOUGAL. Bittersweet.

SARA. You listen.

DOUGAL. Oh, I listen. But I was listening for a song I didn't hear.

SARA. Which?

DOUGAL. "The Best Things In Life Are Free."

SARA. *(a moment)* You came to hear that.

DOUGAL. Yes.

SARA. *(a moment)* No. I didn't sing it.

(She starts to walk. As she does, the doorway slowly recedes off and from the opposite side, a bench with a small tree behind it slowly slides on)

DOUGAL. *(walking with her)* Would you sing it tomorrow night?

SARA. It's not in the set I'm doing.

DOUGAL. Your musicians could play it in their sleep –

SARA. They don't sing it.

DOUGAL. It was my girlfriend's favorite. It made her laugh.

SARA. "The Best Things In Life Are Free" made her laugh?

DOUGAL. She works on Wall Street.

SARA. *(stopping at the bench)* Here's where one of us gets off.

(sits)

DOUGAL. They're not very happy people on Wall Street. It made her happy to laugh. It made me happy to see her happy.

(He sits.)

I had a fantasy I would be listening to you sing "The Best Things in Life Are Free" and she would walk in.

SARA. And laugh.

DOUGAL. She could anything as long as she walked in. The thing about fantasies, you should always remember they're fantasies. She's never going to walk in. She married a short seller.

SARA. Then why do you still want to hear "The Best Things"?

DOUGAL. You made me believe it.

SARA. But it didn't come true for you.

DOUGAL. Not with her. But it will.

SARA. That song means that much?

DOUGAL. Life, she is funny.

SARA. *(after a moment)* Do you believe in coincidence?

DOUGAL. No.

SARA. Don't flirt.

DOUGAL. I don't believe in accidents either. That song means a lot to someone you know, doesn't it?

SARA. Someone I had just met years ago. it was the first song he told me to sing.

DOUGAL. Who was he? Your accompanist?

SARA. *(laughs)* He wasn't even a musician. He had a great ear, though. He was a landscaper. This is his tree. You can't imagine how many bureaucrats he had to work on to get it planted. But he wanted it and here it is – and it's growing. Typical Paolo. He made me grow.

DOUGAL. How?

SARA. The songs he picked – he'd suggest them and say what they meant to him. Making them mean that to me changed how I sang.

DOUGAL. You wanted to do that for a landscaper. Jesus. Why?

SARA. He was Paolo.

DOUGAL. Who was what to you?

SARA. Husband. For 27 years.

DOUGAL. Well, there you have it. My girlfriend lasted a record breaking five.

SARA. His mother says I was fortunate to have had 27 but she's a therapist.

DOUGAL. He had a therapist for a mother and you married him?

SARA. Oh, she paints, too. No lessons. She just began painting flowers, I think it was.

DOUGAL. It usually is.

SARA. But she isn't usual. She began when she got Social Security. Now she can't wait for her patients to go so she can pick up her brushes. He loved her. Really loved her.

DOUGAL. What happened?

SARA. Between her and me?

DOUGAL. Between her and you? She's a therapist, she's your mother-in-law and your husband was mad about her. No. What happened to him?

SARA. *(a long moment)* Colon cancer. Last October 26th, just before midnight.

(a pause)

He was in the hospital and I wasn't there. His doctor had told me he was getting out in the morning so I was home, watering his plants in the greenhouse.

(another pause)

He said you die in hospitals. I hate hospitals. When they called, it was as though they were telling me my order had been cancelled.

DOUGAL. Still, you had 27 years. That's fortunate all right.

SARA. I realized that but it took me too long.

DOUGAL. Well, it meant admitting his mother was right.

SARA. *(laughs)* You certainly say it as it is.

DOUGAL. You don't?

SARA. I don't always know what it is anymore. I talk to Paolo to find out. You believe that?

DOUGAL. Why not?

SARA. Don't flirt.

DOUGAL. I'm not.

SARA. You know why I'm singing again? Bursting into tears was the only way I knew I had any feelings. I could sit with people without hearing a word. I didn't make any effort either. What was the point? I'd had a marvelous marriage to an extraordinary man. He was gone. He wouldn't be back. Then one day, I was watering plants in the greenhouse and there he was. Paolo. We began talking.

(laughs)

SARA. *(cont.)* I washed my hair. Last month, he told me to start singing again. It would help. I've always loved to sing. So I did and he was right. You saw tonight. I'm sort of coming back together. Just as he said I would. Do you believe that?

DOUGAL. Yes.

SARA. Why?

DOUGAL. I believe you.

SARA. Have you lost someone?

DOUGAL. No but my parents lost me when I was born.

SARA. You are flirting.

DOUGAL. I'm not.

SARA. It won't do you any good.

DOUGAL. It would if I were flirting but as it happens, for the moment, I'm not. Look. Either you believe I believe you or you don't.

(a moment)

No. Believe me.

(He takes her hand.)

SARA. *(withdrawing her hand)* Don't.

DOUGAL. You read me wrong.

SARA. I read your basics and I'm trying to help you read me. You know the expression: a hard act to follow?

DOUGAL. Yeah. You know the expression: a good man is hard to find?

(She laughs.)

Thank you! Happy days! There's hope!

(The light fades out.)

Scene Two

(Part of a den converted into a makeshift studio. Water color materials are on an end table next to a tilted board which serves as an easel for the water color **MARION** *is painting on drawing paper pinned to the board. She is a good looking older woman, dressed simply.* **RICHARD** *sits in a large easy chair, trying to pretend he is still the big, tall, attractive man he once was. He plays with a little rubber ball to strengthen his hand.* **MARION** *sometimes pauses mid-sentence for a brush stroke.)*

MARION. So because the song he came to hear her sing is the same song that was Paolo's favorite, a higher power is on the job.

RICHARD. That's what she says.

MARION. Poor Freud.

RICHARD. OK. What would you say it was?

MARION. How about coincidence?

RICHARD. She doesn't believe in coincidence.

MARION. Do you?

RICHARD. I don't believe in believing in anything.

MARION. Yes, I know, but do you believe she began singing again because Paolo told her to?

RICHARD. That's what she said.

MARION. I know that's what she said but do you believe it?

RICHARD. I'm not a believer, I'm a thinker. I think if it makes her happy, he told her to start singing again. What do you think?

MARION. I think it's bullshit.

RICHARD. Surprise!

MARION. Richard –

RICHARD. I will say you're consistent.

MARION. I'm upsetting you.

RICHARD. You are not.

MARION. The doctor warned me not to –

RICHARD. Christ, Marion. I'm fine. I am enormously fine.

MARION. I am enormously pleased.

(as she paints)

Richard, I'm glad she's singing again whatever the reason. It's good for her to be busy doing. It'll help. But sooner or later – sweetheart, Sara has got to accept that Paolo is dead. Then she can move on and get a life going without him.

RICHARD. She accepts that he's dead.

MARION. She does.

RICHARD. Oh, yes.

MARION. She accepts he's dead but she's singing again because he told her to. How did he manage that?

RICHARD. He's Paolo. You wouldn't understand.

MARION. No. I'm his mother.

RICHARD. Well, Sara does. He's here for her.

MARION. Dead but here.

RICHARD. That may seem odd to you but it's not a contradiction. You don't have a drop of poetry in you.

MARION. Thank you for marrying me anyway. Do you accept Paolo's dead?

RICHARD. Every fucking morning.

MARION. Is he here for you?

RICHARD. No.

MARION. But you wish he were.

RICHARD. Lay off, Marion.

MARION. I wish he were but I accept that he's dead and I move on. More patients, more paintings. He's dead, Richard. Not passed away, not gone, not just not here, dead. Merely saying the word helps.

RICHARD. Helps you. You know what helps me? Sara. She keeps him alive.

MARION. For you?

RICHARD. Yes. How about that?

MARION. Good for her. No, you're wrong. I meant that. Anything that helps.

RICHARD. Well, she does.

MARION. And I don't.

RICHARD. It's not your job. I'm your husband, not your patient – at least I hope I'm not.

MARION. I'm not telling.

RICHARD. I'm not paying.

MARION. Richard – he was our son. Feel whatever you have to.

(A moment. She paints.)

RICHARD. OK. What's today's candidate for the Metropolitan?

MARION. Blue horses.

RICHARD. Jesus. Still?

MARION. They're flying now.

RICHARD. Flying. I'd drink to that if I drank.

(a moment)

Why are they flying?

MARION. Why are they blue?

RICHARD. Are you ever going to know?

MARION. I doubt it.

RICHARD. Suppose you were one of your patients?

MARION. I wouldn't go to me.

(SARA walks in.)

I was just about to call you.

(to RICHARD)

That's a coincidence.

(to SARA)

You look lovely, sweetie. I want to ask a favor.

SARA. You look lovely.

RICHARD. *(to SARA)* Ask her your favor.

MARION. She goes first?

RICHARD. She's the best thing that ever happened to Paolo.

MARION. AA was the best thing that ever happened to Paolo.

(to SARA)

Well, he wouldn't have married you otherwise. Or anyone.

(to SARA)

You knew I meant "or anyone," didn't you?

SARA. I knew what you meant, Marion.

RICHARD. OK, girls.

(gets up carefully)

Mickey's on her way over –

MARION. Michelle. Richard, please take it easy.

RICHARD. I'm fine! Michelle's on her way over and the accounts still aren't ready.

(to SARA)

Swap favors with Marion, beauty. Then come by my office and brighten my day.

(He goes.)

SARA. How is he?

MARION. Very well, fingers crossed. Can I ask my favor? I know you're busy again – which is good. Exactly what you need. I mean that. But if I'm asking at the wrong time, just say so.

SARA. No, ask away.

MARION. I did a painting for Paolo's birthday and took it to the framer just before he went to the hospital. Then he died and I forgot all about it. Yesterday, I was looking at my birthday list –

SARA. His is coming up.

MARION. Yes.

(A moment. They're both still.)

Milestones are reminders.

SARA. There's not much that isn't.

MARION. But once you accept –

SARA. What about the painting, Marion?

MARION. It's still at the framer's. Would you mind picking it up for me? I don't want to ask Michelle –

SARA. I don't mind, Marion.

MARION. Why she persists in calling herself Mickey is beyond me. I know it wasn't easy to be Paolo's kid sister. And not being a beauty in the bargain –

SARA. Marion –

MARION. Well, God knows Richard and I didn't help. Frankly, I think she's basically our fault.

SARA. Marion, I said I didn't mind. It's no trouble. I'll pick up the painting.

MARION. Oh. You will?

SARA. Gladly.

MARION. Thank you. I spend so damn much time listening that given half a chance to talk, I can't shut up. The receipt with the framer's address – it's all paid for – here we are.

(hands SARA *the receipt)*

SARA. Where do you want me to bring it?

MARION. Here. Why?

SARA. Well, weren't you going to give it to Paolo for his birthday?

MARION. Yes.

SARA. You still can.

MARION. Oh? And how can I do that?

SARA. Give it to me to hang in his greenhouse.

MARION. Oh, spare me.

SARA. Better than you hanging it here where it would remind Richard.

MARION. *(after a moment)* Name your favor.

SARA. I'd like you and Richard to come hear me sing.

MARION. Sweetie, Richard's in bed by 9:30.

SARA. Truthfully, it's you I'd like to come hear me.

MARION. I can't leave Richard alone.

SARA. Michelle could stay with him.

MARION. I've heard you sing, Sara. Quite a few times.

SARA. To please Paolo.

MARION. Why does it matter now?

SARA. I want you to know me. If you hear me sing, you'll know me.

MARION. I know you, Sara.

SARA. No, you don't, Marion. Even if you ever did, you don't now. I'm different. I sing differently.

MARION. If I hear you, I'll know you and then what?

SARA. You'll let me know you.

MARION. You know me, Sara. You just aren't too fond of what you know.

SARA. Paolo really loved you.

MARION. And you can't figure out why.

SARA. I don't know you.

MARION. But there must be something more to me than what you do know.

SARA. Yes.

MARION. The trust people put in Paolo is frightening. I say that about my own son.

SARA. He was always right about people.

MARION. Heavens. Even his mother? Maybe I should hear you sing.

SARA. He wanted us to love each other, Marion.

MARION. You just blew it.

SARA. Like each other.

MARION. He told you that.

SARA. That's what he wanted.

MARION. He told you that. You heard him.

SARA. *(a moment)* Marion, I didn't leave the house for five months after Paolo died. I didn't sing a note. I didn't answer the phone. I'd go into his greenhouse and burst into tears. I could barely see to water his plants. I didn't know a thing about plants until Paolo but my last anniversary present to him was a rare kind of orchid. Maybe what happened happened because I realized that was our last anniversary. Or maybe it was your department – my unconscious. Anyway – orchids take very little water. That orchid didn't need watering but one day, I lifted the can to pour. I was about to drown it. To kill it in revenge for his death, I guess. Paolo stopped me. He was right there. In the greenhouse. I began talking to him. I know, Marion, but I did. We began having conversations. I started going out of the house, first to buy things for the plants. Then one day, he told me to begin singing again. I did. Even though it was summer and I never sang in summer because that was his busiest time. I like singing warm nights now. I look forward to it. Life's getting better. It would be even better if we were friends, Marion.

MARION. So said Paolo.

SARA. Yes. He did.

MARION. How's the orchid doing?

SARA. Very well, fingers crossed.

MARION. I don't need to hear you sing, Sara.

SARA. Come anyway. You might enjoy it.

MARION. Anything's possible.

SARA. Oh, Marion. You're –

MARION. I always have been.

SARA. Well – I want time with Richard before Michelle arrives.

(She starts out.)

MARION. Sara – aren't you still lonely anyway?

SARA. *(a moment)* I'm a work in progress, Marion. I used to visualize him and cry away. Now I don't let myself visualize him but there are photographs of him – by our bed, on the piano, all over the house. So I cry sometimes anyway. Of course I'm still lonely, Marion. Aren't you?

(The light is fading as she goes.)

Scene Three

(The front of a framing shop.)

(SARA is waiting. She sees an old fashioned bell on the counter. She taps it. A moment after it rings, DOUGAL comes from the back, lugging a picture wrapped in brown paper.)

DOUGAL. Sorry. I was so wrapped up in wrapping this –

(sees her)

Sometimes you're wide awake and it's happening.

(She just stares at him.)

Sara? Sara, you're not going to faint on me?

SARA. This is your shop.

DOUGAL. Yes. Do you want some water? I'll get you a chair.

(He does and seats her as:)

I don't have brandy. You're supposed to for an emergency but so many painters are alcoholics. Sara. Sara, let me –

(She waves him away.)

Sara, I'm harmless.

SARA. *(fishing the receipt from her bag)* You're the framer.

DOUGAL. Yes. Guilty.

SARA. *(handing him the receipt)* This is your receipt.

DOUGAL. *(examines the receipt)* Yep. It's over a year old.

SARA. But you still have the picture.

DOUGAL. Oh yes. One reason I'm still in business. I learned early on: make 'em pay in advance.

(examining the receipt)

It's not a print or a poster.

SARA. How do you know?

DOUGAL. From the price. Do you know what it is?

SARA. A water color, probably.

DOUGAL. Of what?

SARA. Oh, dear. I forgot to ask.

DOUGAL. Any idea?

SARA. No.

DOUGAL. Oy.

SARA. I can't laugh right now.

DOUGAL. No, I meant 'oy' as in trouble. It's a jungle in the back there. I'm not too well organized. Don't worry. As long as you're not in a hurry –

SARA. Blue horses.

DOUGAL. What?

SARA. It might be a water color of blue horses.

DOUGAL. Painted by a beautiful old gal who's a royal pain in the ass.

SARA. Marion.

DOUGAL. I liked her horse painting.

SARA. Can you find it?

DOUGAL. It'll take a little digging. No mat was the right shade of blue for whoever your Marion was having it framed for. The husband was bigger trouble. He laughed at her fussing but he was even more on edge than she was.

SARA. How do you know they were on edge?

DOUGAL. Dougal.

SARA. Dougal?

DOUGAL. Me. That's my name. I wanted to hear you say it.

SARA. Dougal.

DOUGAL. Nice. Thank you. I knew Pa and Ma were on edge the way you know people are on edge when they're on edge. You're on edge.

SARA. I'm not.

DOUGAL. I can hear your heart.

SARA. That's not on edge.

DOUGAL. What do you call it then?

SARA. You came to hear me sing "The Best Things In Life Are Free."

DOUGAL. Yes.

SARA. Paolo's song.

DOUGAL. Yes.

SARA. You're Dougal, the framer.

DOUGAL. Yes.

SARA. That beautiful old woman who painted the blue horses and was so fussy –

DOUGAL. Marion –

SARA. Is Paolo's mother.

DOUGAL. The painter/therapist?

SARA. Yes.

DOUGAL. Holy shit.

SARA. Exactly. That's not the end. She was having it framed for his birthday. By you. I come here to pick up the picture. From you.

(a moment)

Marion would say it's a coincidence.

DOUGAL. It isn't.

SARA. No. It isn't.

DOUGAL. It's Paolo.

SARA. Paolo? Why?

DOUGAL. Bringing us together.

SARA. What?

DOUGAL. He approves of me.

SARA. Is anything else ever on your mind? Sex has nothing to do with this.

DOUGAL. Sex has something to do with everything.

SARA. Not this. This is Paolo.

DOUGAL. I know. I said so.

SARA. You don't know. He isn't only in the greenhouse. He's here. He's with me here.

DOUGAL. Look at your eyes. I always wanted to see someone's eyes light up for me like that. When I was there to see them light up, though. Of course yours did when Paolo was here and could see them. I know: he's here now. But I mean really here – I mean –

SARA. Dougal, you're an attractive man but sex is not where I'm at.

DOUGAL. You think that's the only place I am.

SARA. Yes.

DOUGAL. Wrong. I wouldn't take you if it was only sex.

SARA. Oh, you wouldn't?

DOUGAL. Well, maybe if that's all I could get. But it isn't what I want. It isn't nearly as good. You have to know someone.

SARA. You don't know me.

DOUGAL. I know you well enough from what you sing and how you sing it.

SARA. Well, I don't know you. You don't sing. You're a man who makes frames.

DOUGAL. Yes, I know. You look at me and you see –

SARA. No.

DOUGAL. – some mutt who makes frames –

SARA. No. I see Paolo. No matter who I look at, I see Paolo. I try not to. I know it doesn't help, I know I have to stop but I see Paolo.

DOUGAL. How long ago did he pass away?

SARA. He didn't pass away, he died of cancer.

DOUGAL. Yes. I'm sorry. But it wasn't that long ago, was it? Even so, you can find out what it is about us that Paolo approves of.

SARA. You have a mind like a mountain goat.

DOUGAL. But there is something connecting us. I knew it when we sat on his bench the other night and so did you.

SARA. I knew there was a sexual attraction. Period.

DOUGAL. More.

SARA. No, only.

DOUGAL. More. And today, the minute you saw me here, even more. You know it.

SARA. I haven't even thought about it.

DOUGAL. Well, think about it.

SARA. Dougal, I'm just finding out where I am with myself.

DOUGAL. Whatever this is, it's happening to both of us.

SARA. Repeating doesn't make it true. Paolo and I had a life like no one else.

DOUGAL. You need someone. Everyone does.

SARA. Someone who's dead can mean more than anyone who's living.

DOUGAL. *(a moment)* I'll start hunting the blue horses.

(He starts for the back, then stops and turns around.)

Want something to read while you wait?

SARA. No, I'll be fine.

DOUGAL. Talk to Paolo.

SARA. I might.

DOUGAL. About me.

(The light fades out as he goes off.)

Scene Four

*(The den, late at night. Marion's painting materials have been pushed to one side. A lamp is lit. She sits in the big easy chair, huddled in a light coat. Her back to us, a tall, trousered woman about Sara's age is making drinks. She gives one to **MARION** and sits.)*

MARION. Thank you.

MICHELLE. Aren't you exhausted?

MARION. No.

MICHELLE. Well, you look exhausted.

MARION. Thank you, sweetie.

MICHELLE. It's understandable, you're no spring chicken. How come you called me?

MARION. Under duress. Last time, I barely got him to the emergency room. Your father's a big man no matter how weak these attacks make him. It's no picnic but I wasn't about to risk his life again.

MICHELLE. Whether he wants to or not, he's going to live.

MARION. Come on, Michelle. Enough.

MICHELLE. How many times have you had to up and at 'em?

MARION. How many stents does he have in him?

MICHELLE. Counting tonight?

MARION. No, tonight was another false alarm. Five.

MICHELLE. Why didn't you call me the second time? Or the third?

MARION. You're not going to like this.

MICHELLE. Has that ever mattered before?

MARION. Christ, Michelle.

MICHELLE. Mickey.

MARION. I've never asked you to do anything concerning your father because I know how much you dislike him.

(She stops.)

MICHELLE. Go for it.

MARION. I was unsure whether you might do something – unconsciously, of course –

MICHELLE. Jesus, mother.

MARION. You say what you think, I say what I think. The last thing I wanted to do was call you tonight. But as you pointed out, I'm no chicken. I knew I didn't have the strength to get him to the hospital myself again. I wanted to call Sara but she's doing her show.

MICHELLE. Not this late.

MARION. No, but at the time I wanted to call –

MICHELLE. She was finished.

MARION. She was?

MICHELLE. Yes.

MARION. How do you know?

MICHELLE. She told me the times of her shows. She wants me to come hear her sing.

*(**MARION** laughs.)*

What's so funny?

MARION. Nothing.

(But she laughs again.)

Our Sara must need an audience.

MICHELLE. It has something to do with Paolo, doesn't it?

MARION. Michelle –

MICHELLE. Mickey.

MARION. Not Mickey. Maybe not Michelle, but not Mickey. No matter what gender you go to bed with. I gave both my children special names to give them a head start on being special.

MICHELLE. Think what my life would have been if you'd called me Paolo!

MARION. You more or less are Paolo now. You're his landscaping business .

MICHELLE. Inside the mind of a mother.

MARION. He'd be very proud. You haven't lost one client.

MICHELLE. No, two.

MARION. For Chrissake, Michelle, give yourself your due. And stop making us pay.

MICHELLE. I might do the first but never the second.

MARION. Oh, stop letting resentment cripple your life.

MICHELLE. I'm making another drink. You want one or not? And don't try to twelve step me. You never went after Paolo.

MARION. Is there no limit?

MICHELLE. Apparently not.

(holding out **MARION***'s glass)*

You might as well.

MARION. Famous last words.

MICHELLE. *(making their re-fills)* Not in this family.

MARION. Paolo's dead, he's gone. Forget him.

MICHELLE. Forget him.

MARION. At least try.

MICHELLE. You jest. Try? With a father so obsessed with his fucking beloved son that he had a heart attack the day he died and had to have a coronary by-pass?

MARION. There are coincidences, you know.

MICHELLE. That wasn't one and you know it. Your husband won't let you forget it. Boom! An attack to wake you at one in the morning. Boom! And one more for the wife. Lugging him to the emergency room can't be fun even for you.

MARION. What he has are not heart attacks.

MICHELLE. No. Heart*ache*. That's what he's got. Paolo heartache.

MARION. Don't you miss him?

MICHELLE. What for?

MARION. Even to resent him.

MICHELLE. I don't miss him, I don't resent him. I'm waiting for him.

MARION. You're what?

MICHELLE. Waiting for him. To come back from Lustgarten's.

MARION. What's Lustgarten's?

MICHELLE. His favorite nursery out on the island. As soon as he collects the plants and flowers on his list, he'll come home.

MARION. You're kidding.

MICHELLE. No.

MARION. You're not waiting for him to come back.

MICHELLE. Why not?

MARION. It's out of character. It doesn't make any sense.

MICHELLE. It makes as much sense as Sara singing because Paolo personally told her to. Or daddy having quasi-heart attacks because he's lonely for his boy. Or you pretending to accept your perfect boy is dead and you have to move on.

MARION. *What are you doing?*

MICHELLE. *You're so fucking sure! How do you know what dead is?*

(*A moment, then* **RICHARD** *enters in pajamas and bathrobe.*)

RICHARD. I thought it was a bad dream.

MARION. Go back to bed, sweetheart.

RICHARD. I got out of bed but it didn't go away.

MICHELLE. Sit down, dad.

RICHARD. Oh, I didn't see you.

MICHELLE. Why should this night be any different from all others?

RICHARD. Sara *is* getting smaller checks than she got when Paolo was alive.

(**MARION** *laughs.*)

What's so funny?

MARION. I just love you. Nothing.

RICHARD. Tax returns coming up, that's what did it. They made me face I've been delinquent with the books – have you ever known anyone so long winded? Come on, Dickie boy, get to the point! I couldn't have just a small drink, could I. Do you know what I'd give? Oh, shit. OK, I don't have it to give.

MARION. So the point?

RICHARD. The business hasn't been throwing off as much money as it did when Paolo ran it. Ergo, Sara's checks have been smaller.

(**MICHELLE** *tosses down her drink and walks out.*)

No good night?

MARION. You really don't know why not?

RICHARD. She stands there so fucking unforgiving.

MARION. She's my fault. It was always too obvious I loved Paolo more.

RICHARD. I was even more obvious.

MARION. But you didn't know what you were doing to her and I did.

RICHARD. You must be the first therapist in history who did know what she was doing. Do you resent her?

MARION. God, no.

RICHARD. Why do I?

MARION. Because she's alive and Paolo isn't.

RICHARD. Marion, please. Spare me the Freudian bullshit.

MARION. Is the landscaping really making less money?

RICHARD. Yes.

MARION. Much?

RICHARD. No, but I love him. I'll always love him. She's right to resent him.

MARION. You won't believe what she says she's doing. She says she's waiting for him to come back.

RICHARD. From yonder?

MARION. Oh, she's much more specific. To come back from his favorite nursery out on Long Island where he's buying plants and flowers.

RICHARD. That makes sense.

MARION. It does?

RICHARD. She's afraid he'll come back and put her out of a job she doesn't do as well as he did. Love, Dad. I know why I resent her.

MARION. Why?

RICHARD. Oh, no.

MARION. You can tell me.

RICHARD. The therapist. Oh, sure. I went that route when I was a drunk and look where it got me: into fucking A fucking A.

MARION. Paolo got you into fucking A fucking A, Richard, and AA got us here. We're together.

RICHARD. Without Paolo.

MARION. We have a home together.

RICHARD. What the hey. I resent Michelle because I never wanted a daughter and now that's all I've got.

MARION. Can't it be –

RICHARD. What? You get squirrelly at the oddest times.

MARION. Can't it be home even without Paolo?

RICHARD. Depends what you consider home. But thank you for tonight.

(gets up)

I'm sleepy now.

MARION. Good.

RICHARD. Have a double for me. You deserve it.

(He starts to go off, then turns back.)

Are you going to hear Sara sing?

MARION. No.

RICHARD. Go.

MARION. Because she says Paolo would like it if I did.

RICHARD. Go to enjoy yourself.

MARION. I enjoy myself every day. I paint.

RICHARD. Enjoy yourself with a person for a change.

MARION. I enjoy myself with you.

RICHARD. I'm not very nice, Marion.

MARION. You're nice enough for me.

RICHARD. I can't even remember when I stopped being laughs.

MARION. It isn't for the laughs, Richard. It never was.

RICHARD. Wasn't it? I always wondered what it was for. Well, that was way back anyway Go hear Sara sing.

MARION. For Paolo.

RICHARD. For Paolo, for Sara, for you. Not for me.

(The light fades as he goes off.)

Scene Five

(Part of a greenhouse. Wicker chairs and a table with a watering can and trimming shears. **SARA** *and* **MICHELLE** *examining a multi-colored orchid plant.)*

SARA. Oh, no. Only once a week. You have to be careful not to over-water an orchid.

MICHELLE. Paolo on the Mount.

SARA. Why is there always an edge when you say anything about Paolo?

MICHELLE. There's an edge when I say good morning.

SARA. Do you ever say good morning?

MICHELLE. I don't have time for this. I just came by to explain why your checks are smaller than the ones you used to get from Paolo.

SARA. Who told you they were smaller?

MICHELLE. My father. He should know, he keeps the books.

SARA. Paolo didn't give me checks. Yours are the only ones I've ever gotten.

(a pause)

MICHELLE. Why am I not surprised?

SARA. Paolo took care of everything for me.

MICHELLE. I'm sure he did.

SARA. No, you have no idea. He gave me a credit card. If I wanted cash, I went to a Bible in our bedroom that only looked like a Bible. It was really a cash box passing as the New Testament. He said it was always safe to hide in the Bible. I know you're not listening, you're too busy fuming about your father but I don't think you let yourself know Paolo because you were afraid you might love him.

MICHELLE. Like everybody else.

SARA. Yes, like everybody else.

MICHELLE. You assume.

SARA. No, Michelle, they did and still do.

MICHELLE. People like lovers but you carry on so much about Paolo, you're like an infomercial. I'm sure everybody sympathizes. But do you think people tell you what they think or what you want to hear?

SARA. They love him, Michelle.

MICHELLE. Mickey.

SARA. And he loved you.

MICHELLE. He loved you, Mickey.

SARA. No. Michelle. It's a lovely name. Stop being angry at your mother and your father. You're too old.

MICHELLE. I don't like Michelle, you do. I don't like men, you do. You believe Paolo talks to you, I don't. I don't tell you you're too old to claim you hear him, don't you tell me I'm too old to be angry at a mother and a father whose son had to die so they could discover they also had a daughter. You're as angry as I am only you're angry that Paolo died. Water your orchid and get off it.

SARA. What do you have to water?

MICHELLE. *(a pause)* What do you have to water, Mickey?

SARA. What do you have to water, Mickey?

MICHELLE. His plants.

SARA. Entrusted to the sister he loved, Mickey. The sister he taught to landscape which is why you do it as well as you do, Mickey. The ingrate he trained to take over the business, Mickey.

(The doorbell rings. She calls out:)

It's open!

(to **MICKEY** *again)*

Why can't I believe you don't love your brother?

MICHELLE. Because that's how you keep him alive and that's how everyone helps.

*(***DOUGAL*** *enters carrying the wrapped picture. A moment. All three just stand.)*

DOUGAL. I'm Dougal.

SARA. *(to* **MICHELLE***)* Tell him who you are.

MICHELLE. I'm Paolo's little sister Mickey.

DOUGAL. You do the landscaping now.

MICHELLE. Brought in when he knew he was going to die. The family can't forgive me because I was the one he told he was dying, not them. What idiots. They were better off not knowing. Call me Mickey and we can go bowling together.

(And she goes. A moment.)

DOUGAL. What'd I miss?

SARA. Let's hang the picture.

DOUGAL. In here?

SARA. Yes. Why not?

DOUGAL. You have your heart set on it.

SARA. I'm not porcelain, Dougal. What's wrong with hanging it in here?

DOUGAL. There's too much light for a water color. Those blue horses will fade very quickly.

SARA. This is where I sit and talk with Paolo.

DOUGAL. You think he'll see it.

SARA. Don't start. I've been more than enough for one day.

DOUGAL. OK. He'll see it. He'll love it.

SARA. *(an outburst)* Never mind that she's his sister! Never mind that he knew she resented him and loved her anyway! He trained her to landscape, he taught her how to do everything but love the plants she takes care of. He gave her a life! But she's the only one, the only person who's said anything negative about him since he died! She doesn't believe I sit here and talk with Paolo. She doesn't believe we talk at all. She doesn't believe he's here!

DOUGAL. *(a pause)* Do you really?

SARA. *(a moment)* Do I? I used to be so lonely when I woke up in the morning, I'd wish I never woke up. Now when I wake up, I look forward to the day.

DOUGAL. You're singing again.

SARA. Yes.

DOUGAL. That's your life.

SARA. At the moment. It's wonderful to enjoy again.

DOUGAL. You used to wake up lonely for what?

(She looks at him.)

No, besides that. OK, yes, that, too. Why not? That's life. You're too young not to think about that.

SARA. I never said I didn't think about it.

DOUGAL. But Paolo gets in the way.

SARA. I never said that either.

DOUGAL. He doesn't get in the way.

SARA. In yours, not mine.

DOUGAL. Whoa.

SARA. You want what you can't have. You wanted me to sing a song for someone you could never have. That's why you came to see me, wasn't it?

DOUGAL. Before. That's long over. I want you to sing that song now for me. I'm trying to find out what I can have of you. You'll always love him – 27 years. I know that, I understand that and it hasn't put me off. But I want to know what you've got left for me. Those blue horses will fade whether you hang them in here or not. So will your memories of Paolo. Sara, don't get angry at me for saying that. It isn't going to make it not true. Everything fades. Even someone as extraordinary as your Paolo.

(She is in quiet tears.)

You won't see him so clearly soon enough. You won't hear him so clearly and then hardly at all. Who will you sing for then, Sara?

(The light fades out.)

Scene Six

(The den)

*(**MARION** has been painting; she is in front of her easel. **SARA** and **DOUGAL** are arriving with the wrapped painting, which he holds.)*

SARA. Marion, this is –

MARION. Unnecessary.

DOUGAL. Thank you.

MARION. *(to him)* How could I not recognize you? The hard time you gave me over the color of the mat for my blue horses!

DOUGAL. You're going to be very happy how it turned out.

MARION. *(to **SARA**)* Modest, isn't he?

SARA. Where would you like it?

MARION. Oh, lean it over there somewhere.

SARA. No. I mean where would you like it hung?

MARION. *(a moment)* You wanted it so badly.

SARA. I know but everything's become so unpredictable. What I think I feel one day –

MARION. You don't want it in your greenhouse.

SARA. Dougal says the light there is so bright, the blue horses would fade very quickly.

MARION. And that's the only place in your apartment Paolo could see them.

SARA. If he could see them there, he could see them any place.

DOUGAL. Or not see them any place.

MARION. Not see them?

*(to **SARA**)*

You were so sure.

SARA. That's what I mean. I was, now I'm not.

MARION. What are you sure of?

SARA. Singing.

MARION. Let's not get into that. What else?

DOUGAL. The picture was your birthday present for your
son –

MARION. I was asking Sara.

SARA. I don't know if what I'm sure of today, I will be sure
of tomorrow. But the picture is from you to Paolo so it
should really be here.

MARION. What is it I'm not getting?

SARA. Nothing.

MARION. Something.

DOUGAL. No.

MARION. Yes. And what would you know? You never met
Paolo. You're just the framer.

(*to* **SARA**)

Something's happened.

SARA. Yes but I'm not quite sure what. I sound like an idiot.
I've begun to realize –

MARION. What?

SARA. Things I thought happened – I'm not sure they did.
Like –

DOUGAL. Like did you really hear Paolo tell you to sing.

SARA. Yes, like that. It was what he would do, he would tell
me to sing. I know his voice –

DOUGAL. So you could hear him tell you –

SARA. Oh, what difference whether I really heard him or
not. It was right for me to sing again and I'm so glad
I am!

DOUGAL. Still, pretending is wrong.

SARA. It's not wrong. It doesn't hurt anyone.

DOUGAL. It could.

SARA. Well, maybe I'm not pretending. I might really be
hearing him. How could it hurt anyone?

DOUGAL. There might be things you don't do because you
think Paolo won't like it.

SARA. Oh, there you go.

DOUGAL. No, I don't.

SARA. Dougal –

DOUGAL. No, Sara.

MARION. You know each other. Not from the framing shop. You know each other from before. How do you know each other?

SARA. *(a moment)* He's the one who came to hear me sing "The Best Things in Life."

MARION. Jesus. You must've fallen over when you walked in his shop.

SARA. Almost.

MARION. Coincidence. I said it was all coincidence but now I start wondering if it is just when you start wondering if it isn't. I know where those blue horses came from! When I was little, really little, 4, 5, a carousel arrived in a meadow near our house. I used to stand for hours watching the horses go up and down. I didn't want to ride them, just watch them go up and down. I was so happy. I think it was the happiest I've ever been in my life.

(a pause)

DOUGAL. No wonder the blue horses were your son's birthday present.

MARION. Please. I'm a licensed therapist.

SARA. He's just trying to be helpful.

MARION. *(to DOUGAL)* This has nothing to do with you. He was my son, he was her husband. You just framed the picture. It doesn't affect you.

DOUGAL. It does.

SARA. Dougal –

DOUGAL. Well, it does.

MARION. It does?

DOUGAL. Yes.

MARION. In what way?

(to SARA)

Do you know what he means?

SARA. In a way.

MARION. In a way.

SARA. Yes.

MARION. *(to* DOUGAL*)* I resent you.

(to SARA*)*

This is completely irrational. I don't want you to care about any man except my son.

DOUGAL. That's understandable. She kept him alive for you.

SARA. Dougal –

MARION. *(to* DOUGAL*)* I said I resented you!

SARA. It isn't irrational, Marion, but what you think is not what's going on.

MARION. I don't care what is or isn't or might be. I don't want you to think of any other man than my boy. Of course that's irrational. You're still a young woman. Comparatively. Why don't you sing that goddam song for –

(indicating DOUGAL*)*

him and make him happy? Somebody ought to be happy. Is it impossible without Paolo?

DOUGAL. No.

SARA. Dougal. You don't know.

(to MARION*)*

It all keeps changing and none of us, including Richard and Michelle, can find what to hold on to. If I sang that song, it would be just as much for you as it would be for him.

MARION. Oh, Sara. I come to hear you, we become friends and Paolo is happy. I tell my patients how to deal with loss but I don't know how to be a patient. I think the two of you should go.

SARA. I don't know about becoming friends because I don't know about Paolo and I don't know about you but I know what I need. I need to have someone to talk to about Paolo who knew him and understood him. And that's not Richard or Michelle. It's you. Tell Dougal where you want the picture hung and we'll go. I know I said it might upset Richard to see it but maybe he needs to be shook up. It did Michelle good. It may have done you some good, too.

MARION. Just leave the picture. For the moment.

SARA. Last time, you asked me wasn't I still lonely. I said I was. I still am. But in a very different way. What about you, Marion?

MARION. There are no degrees for me, Sara.

SARA. Aren't you just saying that because that's your style? That's what I'd like to ask but I don't want to alienate you and be cut off.

MARION. We're not friends but I'll call you, Sara. Goodbye, framer.

(**SARA** *and* **DOUGAL** *leave.* **MARION** *stands, looking at the picture she has been working on but not seeing it when* **RICHARD** *walks in.*)

RICHARD. That was the son of a bitch who gave you such a hard time with the mat for your blue horses, wasn't it?

MARION. Yes.

RICHARD. I knew I recognized the prick. Is that the picture?

MARION. Yes.

RICHARD. Where you going to hang it?

MARION. Do you mind if I do?

RICHARD. Not as long as it's someplace I won't have to look at it. I've seen more than enough blue horses for one lifetime. I wish I had your nerve, though.

MARION. Nerve?

RICHARD. To suddenly start painting at a hundred and two. How'd you know you could?

MARION. I didn't. I still don't.

RICHARD. But you don't care.

MARION. No. It's the one thing that gives me joy.

RICHARD. That's what I mean. You have to have a talent for something. Otherwise, you base your life on something and when that's gone, you're gone. Drinking was quintessential. I always wanted to use that word. Quintessential. You have no idea how exhilarating it was to know that once I got drunk – and of course I always could and at so many different speeds – once boozed to the gills, nothing and no one could get to me. Paolo took that away but I didn't mind. I would do anything for him. We got sober together and that brought us even closer. There was nothing to upset or worry me because my boy was there. Then he wasn't and there was nothing. There is nothing. There will always be nothing. I have no talent of any kind. So there it is and here I am, still just keeping the books. Why are you crying, Marion?

(The lights fade out.)

Scene Seven

(The greenhouse.)

*(**SARA** and **DOUGAL** are having drinks. At the moment, she is carefully watering the orchid.)*

DOUGAL. How can anyone be that extraordinary? I take that back. Let me start again. What made Paolo so extraordinary?

SARA. Dougal, I told you to drop it.

DOUGAL. I'm a normal curious human being.

SARA. Normal human beings don't try to compete with a dead man.

DOUGAL. Compete? I'm not trying to compete. I'm not a total clown. I'm just trying to understand.

SARA. Understand what?

DOUGAL. What makes someone desirable to you.

SARA. Dougal, you're you, Paolo was Paolo.

DOUGAL. Humor me. Tell me one thing that made him extraordinary.

SARA. He was the most honest person I ever knew.

DOUGAL. I'm honest.

SARA. Like the rest of us. You went to Patrick, my accompanist, to find out what you could about me.

DOUGAL. Yes. I don't deny it. I want to know everything I can about you. What was wrong with that?

SARA. Nothing. I'm trying to answer you.

DOUGAL. It's so hard for me. I want too much. I know it's too much but I can't stop.

SARA. Dougal –

DOUGAL. Just a footnote. Sorry.

SARA. Patrick was very complimentary, wasn't he?

DOUGAL. Extremely.

SARA. I'm open to suggestions. I'm very considerate of the people I work with. I'm a joy to work with.

DOUGAL. Yes. Quote.

SARA. Did you believe him?

DOUGAL. Of course. Why wouldn't I?

SARA. Paolo would have said: Sara, you pay Patrick.

(a moment)

There was no one like him. He had a twinkle — I'll never love anyone the way I loved him. But Dougal – Dougal, that doesn't mean I can't care for someone else.

DOUGAL. Marry me.

(The doorbell rings three times quickly.)

SARA. That's Michelle. She has her own key but she signals first.

(They wait. Then **MICHELLE** *enters brandishing a gift wrapped bottle.)*

MICHELLE. Champagne. Happy birthday.

SARA. Whose?

MICHELLE. Mine. The champagne's for you. It gives me migraine. It has since I was twelve. This was a present from Mummy and Daddy. But what do you give the girl who won't wear a dress?

(to **DOUGAL***)*

Why didn't you call me?

DOUGAL. I don't bowl.

MICHELLE. I sure know how to pick 'em.

(to **SARA***)*

Around here a lot, isn't he?

SARA. None of your business.

MICHELLE. I'm nervous.

SARA. Why?

MICHELLE. I have to go Lustgarten's. I've kept putting it off but three clients want plants we can only get there. D-Day.

SARA. Why are you nervous about going to Lustgarten's?

MICHELLE. *(a moment)* I'm afraid Paolo's there.

DOUGAL. He's not that extraordinary.

SARA. *(to DOUGAL)* Can you ever not say something?

DOUGAL. I apologize, Mickey.

(She flips her hand in acknowledgement.)

SARA. Have a drink.

MICHELLE. Not on the job.

SARA. It's your birthday.

MICHELLE. Your late husband never drank on the job. Even on the days when he never ate after sundown. He would never have a drop in him when he entered a client's house – only they didn't think of themselves as clients, they were his friends. He was visible to every single one of them. Michelle who?

SARA. *(murmurs)* Excuse me.

(and leaves with the champagne)

DOUGAL. You have to go to that plant place but you believe Paolo is there and that makes you afraid. Afraid of who doing what, Mickey?

MICHELLE. You're not only a smartass, you're an ignorant smartass and your ignorant smartass deduction is a cliché. Life ain't so simple, Junior.

DOUGAL. Not to all you Paolo worshippers but it could be if you brought him down to planet earth and relaxed.

(SARA comes back with a plate holding a brownie with a single little candle burning on it.)

SARA. Happy birthday.

MICHELLE. Oh, Sara.

SARA. Make a wish.

MICHELLE. Will it come true?

SARA. Yes. Absolutely.

MICHELLE. *(ready to blow out the candle but she waits)* I don't know what to wish for.

DOUGAL. A lover.

SARA. Oh, yes. Wish for love, Mickey.

MICHELLE. *(blows out the candle)* I didn't. I couldn't make myself. I wished Paolo wouldn't be there. Go easy on the cake.

(She goes. Then:)

DOUGAL. Well?

SARA. Why?

DOUGAL. If you marry me, I'll know you care enough.

SARA. I'll never care as much as you'd like.

DOUGAL. I know that.

SARA. No, you don't. You think you do but you always have your fantasies. And sex has given you false hopes.

DOUGAL. This has nothing to do with sex.

SARA. Dougal, you said everything has to do with sex.

DOUGAL. Yes, but not this.

SARA. It does. No – hush and listen. When Paolo died, sex died with him. It didn't exist for me. I thought it never would again. Then one night –

DOUGAL. – you met me.

SARA. *(laughs)* A little earlier than that. The night I started to sing again. Music is life to me and sex is part of life so there I was, back to life and *then* I met you. I was attracted to you, Dougal. Sex matters to me. I enjoy it but it has nothing to do with Paolo. What I felt for him, I still feel, I'll always feel. Love. The only love I'll ever feel no matter how long I live.

DOUGAL. So sex with me is just sex? I don't believe it.

SARA. That isn't what I meant. You make up meanings that make you a victim. I'm not capable of having sex without feeling. I do care for you, Dougal. But it's more 'like' than 'love'. Affection. Real affection but that's all. And all it'll ever be.

DOUGAL. You don't know that.

SARA. I know it's always going to be less than you want. Fantasies can come true – you're very good at persuading yourself. I don't want to stand in the way of you getting what you want.

DOUGAL. You couldn't. You are the fantasy and you have come true. Not completely, not yet, but you will –

SARA. No.

DOUGAL. You've changed already. You said so yourself.

SARA. No, Dougal.

DOUGAL. You were so sure you heard him tell you to sing.

SARA. No No No. What you can't get through your head is that I am still happy with Paolo. I don't know if you can understand how it works – it may sound bizarre – but the more his memory fades, the farther away I get from suddenly brimming with tears, then the happier I am remembering what I had. I couldn't have done better. I don't think anyone could. I know that's the past and I would like a present. It can't be what I had and it can't be what you want. I know that, too. I want you to know it.

DOUGAL. You live in the past. I live in the now.

SARA. I live in both, Dougal.

DOUGAL. *(a pause)* One of us could make the other happier.

SARA. Happier?

DOUGAL. Happy is one fantasy I don't have.

SARA. *(a pause)* You're a very sweet man.

DOUGAL. *(walking away from her)* I don't want be dismissed as 'sweet'. 'Sweet' gets you nowhere!

SARA. It keeps getting you closer and closer.

(She goes to him and they really kiss.)

I have to change for my show.

DOUGAL. I'll clean up.

SARA *(off)* Just leave everything.

DOUGAL. No, I want to clean up. The longer I stay, the longer I'm with you.

(He is collecting the glasses when the doorbell rings: **MICHELLE***'s signal. Then she comes in.)*

MICHELLE. Forgot my cell.

(picks it up)

I'm not nervous. Thanks to you, swain.

DOUGAL. Because I'm sweet.

MICHELLE. Sweet? Sweet went out with the stock market. I haven't known anyone sweet in years. What are you thinking?

DOUGAL. You were always ahead of your time.

MICHELLE. Say it, Junior. You can say anything to me. No, I wasn't thanking you for being what no one is anymore, I'm too avant garde. I was thanking you for knocking one impossibility out of my head and replacing it with a more palatable one.

DOUGAL. Love is an impossibility?

MICHELLE. For me, it is.

DOUGAL. You can't let it be. It's the best thing in life.

MICHELLE. Not for the likes of us, buster. Perk up! Everybody does with less. Nobody has it all.

DOUGAL. Sara did.

MICHELLE. Did. Past tense. Keep chugging, framer.

(She goes. He cleans up, starts to leave, stares at the orchid on his way, then goes as:)

(The light fades out.)

Scene Eight
Sara

*(Music and in the darkness, **SARA** singing:)*

SARA.

Life – life – life is just a bowl of cherries.

(She comes into view , singing into a microphone as earlier, in that little black dress with a spotlight on her. But her tone this time is cheerier, brighter:)

Don't take it serious
It's too mysterious.
You work, you slave, you worry so
But when the end comes around
You have to go go go

(The music continues but she stops, smiles, looks out into the club and then holds up her hand to her musicians and sings:)

The moon –

(They stop playing. She continues a cappela.)

belongs to everyone –

(On that last, the music comes back in with her.)

The best things in life are free
The stars belong to everyone
They cling there for you and me

The flowers in spring
The sunbeams that shine
The robins that sing
They're yours, they're mine

Love can come to everyone
The best things in life are –

(joyously)

Flowers in spring
Robins that sing

Sunbeams that shine
They're all yours, they're mine!

For love can come to anyone
It's the best thing in life
And the best things in life
Are free.

(The light fades out swiftly.)

Scene Nine
The bench by the tree

(**MARION**, *well groomed, is sitting on the bench in the moonlight, singing a cappella:*)

MARION. *(singing)*
> "The sunbeams that shine,
> they're yours…
> Their mine. For love can come to everyone"…

(She sits, thinking. **SARA** *comes on, a jacket over her dress and sits down.)*

MARION. I never really heard you before. You're good.

SARA. Thank you. I'm singing differently.

MARION. I wouldn't know. I didn't listen before.

SARA. Why not?

MARION. Long story.

SARA. Marion, I was very glad you came. I was singing for you.

MARION. And Dougal.

SARA. For you first.

MARION. But to make him happy.

SARA. Happier.

MARION. Who made that distinction?

SARA. Dougal.

MARION. He's more than sexy.

SARA. Oh, yes. It wasn't hard to make him happier. It would be hard with you. I didn't even try. I just wanted to get through to you. Why do you make it so hard?

MARION. *(after a moment)* Love doesn't come for everyone, Sara. That's just a song. You sing it well because it comes from inside you. That comes from what you had with Paolo.

SARA. At least tell me why you listened tonight and heard me and couldn't or didn't when you came with Paolo.

MARION. *(a moment)* I was too angry.

SARA. At me.

MARION. No, dear Sara. Because of you.

SARA. Oh. Me and Paolo.

MARION. Yes.

SARA. But why? Not because he loved me.

MARION. Yes.

SARA. But you knew he did. You seemed happy he was going to marry me.

MARION. I was.

SARA. Then what?

MARION. I had never watched him listen to you sing. It was like watching the two of you in bed. You want a distinction? Between his love for you and his love for me. *That's* a distinction. It made me very angry.

SARA. I'm sorry.

MARION. It's me, Sara, not you, not Paolo – me.

SARA. Marion…

MARION. Go for it, Sara. I'm formidable.

SARA. I don't want to say anything to hurt you.

MARION. If you don't mean to hurt, then you won't hurt.

SARA. Do you say that to your patients or do you believe it?

MARION. I say it to my patients and I hope it's true. I think it will be with you.

SARA. …A few weeks before Paolo died, he blew up at Michelle about something she had done at Lustgarten's. They both felt terrible. She ran out of the greenhouse and then he told me what he'd been letting out on her was sideways anger. Do you know what that is?

MARION. A term he picked up in AA.

SARA. It wasn't really Michelle he was angry at. What he was angry at was the cancer that was killing him. That was how he told me he was dying.

(a moment)

SARA. *(cont.)* He didn't want anyone else to know, least of all you. He said he wasn't worried about me because I would somehow find a way to make a life. He was very worried about you, though. He said you only seemed contained and controlled –

(She smiles.)

"Formidable," as you call it. But that was just a persona you had invented for yourself years ago.

(She waits.)

MARION. Go on.

SARA. He said his death would be harder on you than anyone and would I take care of you.

MARION. Did he say why he thought that?

SARA. No.

MARION. *(a moment)* He really loved me. I mean I knew – but he really did.

SARA. Very much.

MARION. But he was the only one who did. What you and he had together, I never had. Maybe at the beginning Richard and I came close but if we did, it wasn't for long. The only person Richard has ever really loved was Paolo.

SARA. But you haven't given up.

MARION. You noticed. No, I haven't. I can't. I keep dragging him to the hospital because maybe there will be one of those last minute conversions. Do you watch TV?

SARA. Not much. But everybody hopes.

MARION. Are you going to marry Dougal?

SARA. He wants me to.

MARION. You don't love him.

SARA. No but I like him.

MARION. Enough to marry him?

SARA. I don't know.

MARION. Enough to go to bed with him?

SARA. I have.

MARION. Already?!

SARA. It was a possibility the first night we met.

MARION. Despite Paolo?

SARA. It has nothing to do with Paolo.

MARION. Sex with someone else has nothing to do with the man whose death devastated you. It exists by itself in a bubble.

SARA. Pretty much.

MARION. You care about it just for itself.

SARA. Yes. Don't you?

MARION. Not much. I never have. I must be missing a gene or two. Is this what being friends is? Talking about sex?

SARA. Talking about anything and everything. I don't really know. I've never had a real friend. Except Paolo.

MARION. I've never had a friend. Too busy being a paid friend to patients.

SARA. Not Paolo?

MARION. I could never tell him what I just told you. Richard is his father.

SARA. Well, now you have a friend.

MARION. Sara. How can we be friends? What do we have in common? We're different generations. We lead very different lives. Yes, there is one thing we do have in common: we both loved an extraordinary boy who was my son and your husband. But he's *dead. (she almost breaks down)* I'm sorry to put it like that, Sara.

SARA. If you don't mean to hurt, you don't. You didn't. How are you dealing with the loss, Marion?

MARION. I thought I was doing fine and dandy but I was kidding myself. Now I'm — well, I don't quite know how to deal with it.

SARA. That's why you need a friend.

MARION. You might, I don't.

SARA. Yes, you do! I know I do! We both do! We both have an emptiness that will never go away. We need each other, Marion. We both need a friend who loved Paolo and can help us keep him alive. He has to be kept alive or the emptiness will swallow us!

MARION. But you're only my friend because Paolo asked you to be.

SARA. That's what started me off but it turned tonight.

MARION. How?

SARA. *(a moment)* I like you. Marion.

MARION. *(a moment)* Why?

SARA. You talked to me.

MARION. Just talking did it?

SARA. Yes.

MARION. Pity I don't sing.

> *(They both laugh.)*

> What does a friend do?

SARA. Listens and talks. Isn't that what you do every day?

MARION. No. I listen and don't talk. Certainly never about me.

SARA. But you did to me two minutes ago. Didn't it make you feel good?

MARION. At the moment. Now I wish I hadn't.

SARA. Why? What are you afraid of?

MARION. The Empress's new clothes! Love is not the best thing in my life.

SARA. It's just a song, Marion.

MARION. No! It's a belief! You sing that it's the best thing in life. My patients say it. Paolo said it. I can't because I've never had it. You know that and I wish you didn't.

SARA. But that makes me want to be your friend even more. I need you, Marion. We need each other. You have to be my friend.

> *(A moment. Then from the club, the distant sound of the piano and bass playing "The Best Things in Life.")*

MARION. Is love really free?

SARA. No. Friendship isn't either.

MARION. That's all right.

SARA. Do you mean that?

MARION. I expect nothing is free.

SARA. Then we're friends?

MARION. Well, we might be.

SARA. No. We are. We have to be.

MARION. Then we are, Sara.

SARA. Oh, Marion! I feel almost happy!

(The piano and bass play on as...)

(The light fades out.)

Also by
Arthur Laurents...

The Radical Mystique

The Time of the Cuckoo

OTHER TITLES AVAILABLE FROM SAMUEL FRENCH

THE RADICAL MYSTIQUE

Arthur Laurents

Drama / 3m, 2f / Interior

In the New York of the late 60's when the term "radical chic" was coined by Tom Wolfe, friends Josie and Janice are arranging a party to aid the Black Panthers' Self Defense Fund. In the process, their complacency is shaken and they are forced to confront things they would prefer to leave alone.

"Achingly earnest comedy of manners...His concern is nothing less than the way in which the most basic relationships are sustained by lies."
– *The New York Times.*

"It holds the interest in the old fashioned way. It earns it."
– *New York Post*

"Full of Laurents' caustic wit and moments of wisdom...An unusually civilized evening."
–*New York Daily News*

OTHER TITLES AVAILABLE FROM SAMUEL FRENCH

GATES OF GOLD

Frank McGuinness

Drama / 3m, 2f / Interior

Written by acclaimed Irish author Frank McGuinness, whose *Someone Who'll Watch Over Me* earned a Tony Award nomination, *Gates of Gold* is an acerbic duel between two lovers, the fashionable and eloquent theatrical trailblazers who founded Dublin's Gate Theatre. *Gates of Gold* is witty and moving – a vibrant celebration of art, love, and finally, life itself.

"Compelling! This endearing love letter of a play!"
– *The New York Times*

"Moving! Provocative! Compelling performances!"
– *New York Post*

www.ingramcontent.com/pod-product-compliance
Lightning Source LLC
Chambersburg PA
CBHW070417120726

47909CB00005B/1679